For Daniel William and Adam Joshua,
brothers and best friends!
—A.S.C.

HarperCollins®, 🐾, and I Can Read Book® are trademarks of HarperCollins Publishers Inc.

Library of Congress Cataloging-in-Publication Data

Capucilli, Alyssa Satin.
   Biscuit's day at the farm / story by Alyssa Satin Capucilli ; pictures by Pat Schories.—1st ed.
      p.   cm.
   ISBN-10: 0-06-074167-8 (trade bdg.) — ISBN-13: 978-0-06-074167-9 (trade bdg.)
   ISBN-10: 0-06-074168-6 (lib. bdg.) — ISBN-13: 978-0-06-074168-6 (lib. bdg.)

2006000562
CIP
AC

18 SCP 10 ❖ First Edition

I Can Read!

SHARED **My First** READING

Biscuit's Day at the Farm

story by ALYSSA SATIN CAPUCILLI
pictures by PAT SCHORIES

HarperCollins*Publishers*

Come along, Biscuit.
We're going to help
on the farm today.

Woof, woof!

We can feed the hens, Biscuit.

Woof, woof!

We can feed the pigs, too.

The pigpen
is empty, Biscuit.
Where can the pigs be?

11

Woof, woof!

Funny puppy.

You found the pig
and the piglets, too.
Woof!

Let's feed the goats,

Biscuit.

Woof, woof!

Oink!

Oh, Biscuit.

The piglet is out of the pen.

We must put
the piglet back.
Woof, woof!

Let's feed the sheep, Biscuit.
Woof, woof!

Oink!

Oh no, Biscuit.

It's the piglet!

We must put the piglet back
one more time.
Woof, woof!

19

Here are the geese,
Biscuit.

Woof, woof!

Oink!

Here is the piglet again.

Woof, woof!

Oink! Oink!

Honk!

Wait, Biscuit!

The geese are just

saying hello.

Woof!

Silly puppy!
The piglet is back
in the pen.

And so are you, Biscuit!

Oink!

Woof, woof!